To Diane

who knows that no
experience is wasted
and that any past can
be healed.

There is a
friend who sticks closer
than a brother.
PROVERBS 18:24

Once upon a time a very sad thing happened.
VERY SAD.

My mommy became an alcoholic. PLEASE don't tell anybody I told you. Most people don't understand.

Some days when I come home from school Mommy is sleeping. She's drunk. That's why. The front door is locked, so I sit on the steps and wait till Daddy comes home. I could wake her up but she'd be mad.

What if Daddy doesn't come home tonight?

Daddy is proud of me because I am so grown up. I do lots of things other kids can't, like cook supper and wash clothes. I know it helps Daddy. Our house is messy and dirty.

The refrigerator is almost empty.

Some food is rotten.

The closet stinks.

And yucky bugs called cockroaches live in our kitchen.

I wonder what I could do to make Mommy stop drinking?

Laura, my little sister, is always trying to help Mommy feel happy. She pats her, and once she said, "Don't worry, Mommy, we don't need to have you take care of us."

I wish I could invite Nicole to come over and play, but I would be embarrassed. Sometimes I feel disgusted when Mommy passes out and wets her pants, and sometimes I feel better when that happens because it PROVES she's sick.

Why does Daddy
say everything
is fine?

My mommy drinks Scotch. She gulps Scotch. She drinks a lot of it before she gets drunk.

I have so many questions, but I don't want to talk to Daddy because he is so sad and tired and worried, so I talk to my dolly, whose name is Friend.

Why does Daddy put up with this? I asked Friend.

"Because in spite of her drinking, Elizabeth, he still loves her."

On Thanksgiving Day we went to Grandma's. I took Friend and sat by myself. Pretty soon Friend said:

"You may feel lonely, Elizabeth, but you are not alone. Millions of children have an alcoholic parent.

"And what's more, it doesn't matter HOW many times your mom tells you, 'If it weren't for you I wouldn't be drinking.' You are NOT the cause of your mom's alcoholism."

Friend, I'm so glad you understand, because I'm the only one in my family who knows my mother is an alcoholic. Nobody ever talks about it.

Mommy isn't out of bed in the morning when I go to school. Last week, when we had our Christmas program, I wore the dress Grandma made. It was very cold outside and my teacher said, "Elizabeth, does your mother know you didn't wear a coat? Can't you see all the children have wool sweaters and pants on?"

I said, "Oh, my mommy told me to dress warmly, but I forgot."

Then I remembered that Friend said, *"It's OK to tell the truth; you don't have to cover up for your mom."*

When the program started, I looked for Daddy. He said he would come but he didn't. Just then, Mommy came. She was talking real loud and couldn't find a seat. Everybody looked. Nicole said, "Is she DRUNK?" Everybody heard her say it.

Daddy called Mommy's boss again and said she "has the flu" and can't come to work. The truth is she's drunk.

Friend, why can't Mommy stop drinking? And Friend said, "*She is afraid to stop. She feels awful inside when she does not drink.*"

Laura says Mommy drinks because her
best friend moved away and because
her boss is mean and because she needs
it for her "nerves." She says Mommy
loves us, so she couldn't be an alcoholic!

I say she drinks because
she's sick inside herself.

I took money from Mommy's purse today when she was sleeping so I could buy groceries for the family. It made me feel guilty, but I know there is no food left.

Sometimes Mommy says it is OK to take money for food, and sometimes she gets real mad. I never know what she will say.

When I came home, Mommy was walking around the house with her blouse unbuttoned and the zipper open on her pants. I don't like it when she's not covered up.

"Tell her," Friend said. *"Tell her you don't like it."*

When Mommy is yelling, Daddy says she's not mad, she's just "explaining things." And when she doesn't take care of my little sister it's not because she is drunk, she's just "teaching her to be independent." Sometimes when I obey I get yelled at, and sometimes Mommy says I am a good girl.

It is VERY confusing.

Mommy likes Laura better than me because she never gets mad when Daddy or Mommy don't keep their promises.

Friend said, *"Elizabeth, you have heard many promises and have been disappointed. You don't have to pretend it's no big thing. Any ten year old would feel just like you feel."*

Friend, I know how to get my mom to stop drinking. I'll tell her when I smell booze on her breath or when she's walking funny, and I will dump all the alcohol down the toilet.

"No, Elizabeth, she would tell you to mind your own business and then be angry with you. There is NOTHING you can do to make her stop drinking."

Mommy is drinking again. I had to walk home from Nicole's house because she forgot to come and get me. I feel guilty for hating someone I'm supposed to love and I feel guilty for being ashamed of my mother.

Sometimes Mommy is not drinking and then she cooks supper. She makes vegetables. I hate peas! When I cook, we have cereal and cookies and peanut butter on toast.

And, Friend, Mommy and Daddy don't TALK to me. They leave money on the kitchen table when I need it, but they don't *talk* to me. Doesn't Mommy love me?

"Right now, your mother is not capable of loving you, or herself," Friend said.

Last night I cooked a special
supper. We had wieners and
ice cream. I waited for
Mommy to come home.
When she came home she
was drunk and she went
straight to bed. Then she got
up in the night. I could hear
the ice cubes—sometimes
her hands are shaky and she
spills.

Sometimes at night I can't sleep because there is so much yelling and screaming and shouting and crying.

Friend said, *"Elizabeth, honey, don't disagree with your mommy when she is drunk. And when your daddy says, 'Who do you think is right?' don't take sides. If you don't take sides maybe they will get help sooner."*

Last night Daddy hit Mommy and called her a "drunk." Mommy kicked Daddy. Laura and I ran next door.

Mrs. B said, "The police should lock your mom up and throw away the key." It hurt my feelings. We don't need help. I can do everything. That night I decided to write down the rules:

Rule #1 - Supper time is 6:00 P.M.
Rule #2 - Nobody plays on Saturday 'til the house is cleaned.
Rule #3 - Laura cleans the turtle box.
Rule #4 - Elizabeth cooks, buys groceries, washes clothes.
Rule #5 - We don't tell nobody our mom's an alcoholic.

We looked at magazines 'til we got
sleepy. Laura said, "How come they
show pictures of people drinking
alcohol who look happy and beautiful
and rich? Drinking booze just makes
you drunk!"

And we looked at pictures of houses that
were pretty and clean and where everyone
smiled. Laura said, "Do some people live
like that?" And I said, "I don't know.
Maybe."

When it was quiet,
Friend began to talk.
He said,

"*Tell your mother that you are hurting because she is an alcoholic, and that you need someone to help you, even if she doesn't get help for herself. It will probably make her angry because she will feel guilty. You can be in charge of getting help by telling a loving grown-up what is happening at your house.*"

Friend continued,

"Not everyone will understand. Some people will be unkind out of ignorance, some will avoid you because they are afraid or critical. But some adults will quietly love you and be there. I know you don't care how you're treated at home as long as outsiders don't find out . . .

but

it's time now to tell somebody the truth."

I am so scared when Mommy drives drunk. Today she did not stop at the red light, and she hit another car. An old man was hurt very badly. There was lots of blood. The police took Mommy away.

Finally, Mommy went to a special hospital for alcoholics. Daddy said she would stay there about one month.

Daddy said, "Your mom was not able to stop drinking no matter how sorry she was about it. She COULDN'T stop by herself. She needed help."

I said, "Will Mommy get better at the hospital?" And Daddy said, "No one knows for sure."

When I got home, Friend was waiting. He wrapped his floppy arms around me and his button eyes cried real tears.

"You have become a mother to your mother. Even if she does not stop drinking, you can be happy. There is nothing you can do to make her stop. Right now, drinking is more important to your mother than anything else."

I said, "NO, NO! She loves me more than booze!" Friend just hung his head.

When he could talk again he said,

"There will be some hard days ahead when your mom comes home from the hospital. She may be very strict to make up for the times she was not in control. And she may go to meetings every night. Even if she is not drinking she won't be there for you for a while."

I will wait, Friend.
I will wait.

Dear Friend,

The following suggestions are offered to help a child understand that no one needs to be the victim of his past. The good, helpful behavior of the child of an alcoholic becomes a burden to him as an adult.

Children can be told that . . .

1. Alcoholism makes people unable to control their drinking.
2. They NEED someone to talk to. It is a fortunate child who has a best friend.
3. Many children of alcoholics need to learn to cry. Expressing feelings is hard work for the child of an alcoholic parent.
4. Expressing feelings develops closeness, and that is scary, too.
5. They do not have to explain to friends they bring home that their parent is an alcoholic.